if i had a DRACON

Written and illustrated by Tom and Amanda Ellery

SIMON AND SCHUSTER
London   New York   Sydney

To our parents, who inspired us when we were young, and to our three
Mortons - Tommy, Johnny, and Katie - who inspire us today.

And to Alisha Niehaus and Daniel Roode - for making it happen.

SIMON AND SCHUSTER

First published in Great Britain in 2007 by Simon & Schuster UK Ltd

Africa House, 64-78 Kingsway, London WC2B 6AH

A CBS company

Originally published in 2006 by Simon & Schuster Books for Young Readers,

an imprint of Simon & Schuster Children's Publishing Division, New York

Copyright © 2006 by Tom and Amanda Ellery

Book design by Daniel Roode

The text for this book is set in Albatross

The illustrations for this book are rendered in charcoal, ink and watercolour

A CIP catalogue record for this book is available from the British Library

ISBN 1 416 92637 2

ISBN-13 9781416926375

Printed in China

10 9 8 7 6 5 4 3 2 1

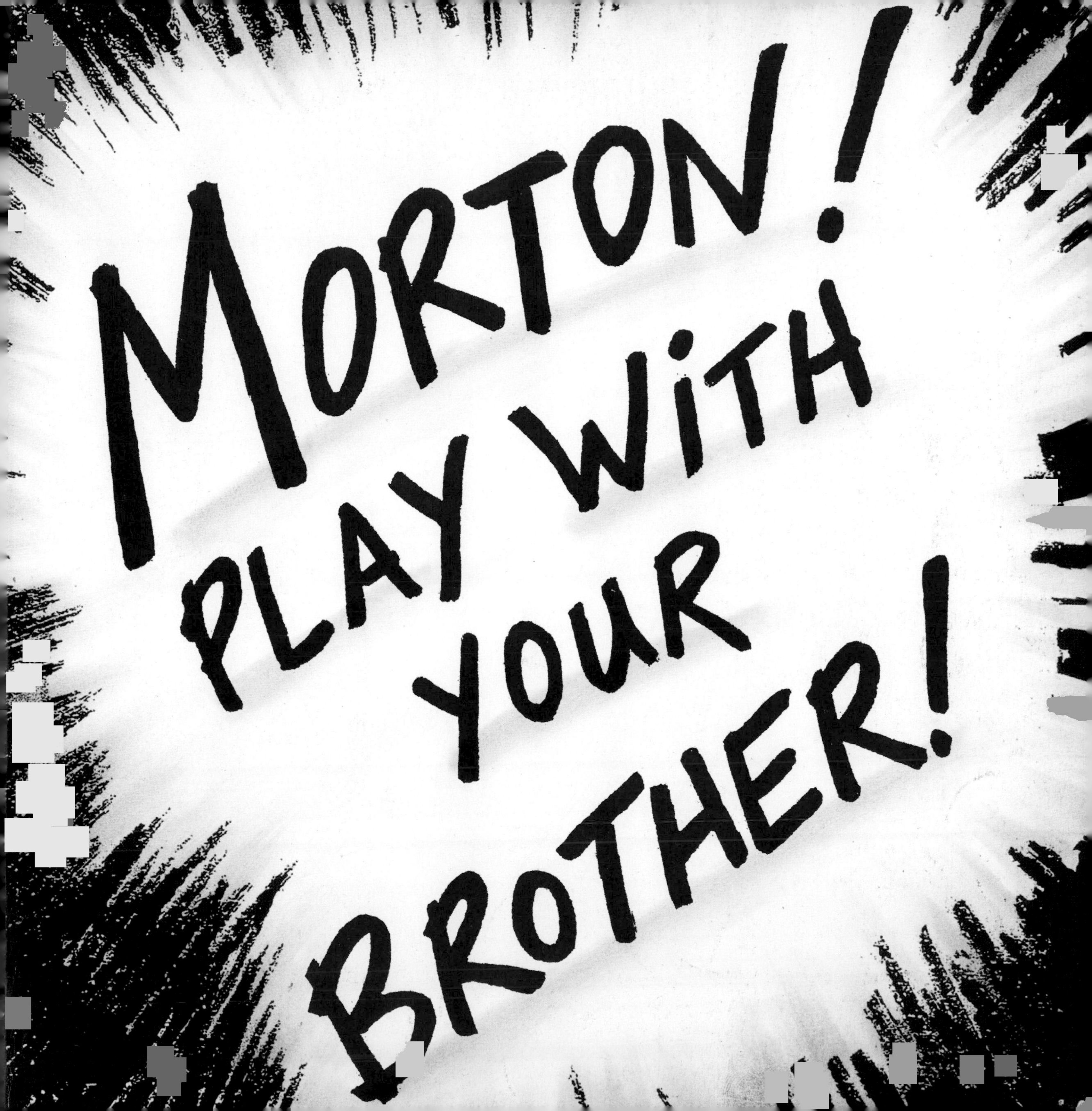
MORTON! PLAY WITH YOUR BROTHER!

I don't want to play with my brother! He's too little.

I wish he would turn into something fun . . .

...a DRAGON!

If I had a dragon, I would be so happy. We could go for walks. . .

We could play basketball!

Oh.

Go for a swim?

OUCH!

Play hide-and-seek?

28 . . .
29 . . .
30!

Ready or not, here I . . .

. . . come.

A movie?

WHISTLE?

I guess a dragon doesn't make a very good playmate after all.

You go home!